W9-ALN-145

The Chain

by
Anne Schraff

Perfection Learning Corporation

Logan, Iowa 51546

Cover Illustration: Greg Hargreaves

For information, contact:
Perfection Learning Corporation
1000 North Second Avenue, P.O. Box 500,
Logan, Iowa 51546-0500.
Tel: 1-800-831-4190 • Fax: 1-800-543-2745

RLB ISBN-13: 978-0-7569-0289-6
RLB ISBN-10: 0-7569-0289-4
PB ISBN-13: 978-0-7891-5510-8
PB ISBN-10: 0-7891-5510-9
6 7 8 9 10 11 PP 12 11 10 09 08 07
perfectionlearning.com
Printed in the U.S.A.

1 "Letter for you, Catie," Catie Rezo's mother said as she walked in the front door. She set a business-sized envelope on the coffee table.

Curious, Catie paused in the middle of her algebra homework to check out the letter. She didn't get much mail except from her grandfather in Florida. She used to get letters from her pen pals in Israel and Mexico, but since they all had access to the Internet now, using the post office had become obsolete. Instead, they sent messages via email.

Catie picked up the envelope. There was no return address, and she didn't recognize the handwriting. She spied her mom's ivory-handled letter opener on the coffee table. Grabbing it, she ripped open the envelope. The letter had been printed on a computer, so there was no handwriting to analyze either.

"Dear Catie," she read aloud, "this is not a chain letter, but it might remind you of one. It is very important that you make five copies of this letter, including the following poem. Send them to friends and relatives within five days. Do not break this chain or you will face dire consequences.

Fireflies glow and eagles fly,
Coyotes howl to a moonlit sky,
Betrayal, treachery, dreams that die,
Are often the lot of you and I."

Catie laughed. "How stupid," she said.

"It says it's not a chain letter, but it is," her mom said. "All these things are the same. They try to frighten you into keeping them going. I never pay any attention to them. Some weird people think they really affect our futures, but that's nonsense. Just throw it away, sweetheart," she said.

Catie's little sister, Leslie, was sitting by her on the couch. She grabbed the letter from her sister and read it. Giggling, she said, "I got one of these last year. My friend Paula and I both did. It was from a kid in our class. We did what it told us to do. It was kinda fun. I read somewhere that a chain letter kept going for five years and nobody broke it. Then somebody broke it, and he fell down the stairs and broke both his legs."

"Oh, Leslie," said her mom, "you surely don't believe things like that, do you?"

Leslie shrugged. "I don't know. I saw a movie once where somebody broke a chain letter and—"

"Come on, Leslie, don't be silly," Mrs. Rezo scoffed. "Just toss it in the round file, Catie."

Catie looked at the letter again. "I wonder what weirdo at Marshall sent this to me," she said.

"It's kind of a cool poem though," Leslie said.

"Yeah, whatever," Catie said.

"I bet your boyfriend, Todd, sent it," Leslie said. "He's always talking about weird stuff when he comes over, like karma and the universe."

"Oh, Todd wouldn't do that," Catie said firmly. "And he's *not* my boyfriend, Leslie. We've gone out a couple of times, but that's it."

Todd Hubbard was a senior, one year older than Catie. He was very smart and also a great athlete. He was a computer whiz, and he spent his free time designing Web pages. And it was true, he did have an open mind about a lot of far-out ideas. But Catie admired that.

Catie wouldn't have minded calling Todd her boyfriend, but she wasn't sure he felt the same way. She didn't want it getting around that she thought there was something there if Todd felt different. That would be way too embarrasing.

Catie got up from the couch and tore the letter in half. She tossed it in the trash and then went back to her homework. Leslie went to her room to listen to a new CD.

Half an hour later Catie's dad came home. He owned his own electrical company. Catie knew they were pretty lucky. They had a lot more money than most of her friends.

"Hey, Dad," Catie said, "how's everything?"

"I'm tired," her dad said with a weary smile. "Everything that could go wrong went wrong today." He sat down in front of the television and turned on the early evening news. Then he glanced at Catie. "School okay?"

"Yeah, I'm studying for a math test tomorrow," Catie answered. "It's going to be bad. Ms. Bricker is like a drill sergeant at boot camp. She's turning me against math."

"Don't let her do that," Mr. Rezo said, his attention already on the news program he was watching.

Catie loved her father, but she wasn't close to him. Leslie had a much better relationship with their dad. Catie was closer to their mom. It was funny too, because Catie looked liked her mom, while Leslie resembled their father.

Leslie ran into the living room as she always did when her dad came home. She sat on the edge of her dad's chair and said, "Know what, Dad? Catie got a chain letter today. A *real* chain letter. Is that cool or what?"

"I threw the stupid thing away," Catie said.

"It was a little bit threatening," Mrs. Rezo added, walking in from the kitchen to give her husband a peck on the lips. "It had all sorts of nonsense in it about treachery and betrayal, and, of course, dire things would happen if the chain was broken."

"I'm glad you tossed it, Catie," her dad said. "It can really freak you out when you start taking junk like that seriously. It's like looking into crystal balls and reading palms. Psychics predicting the future and all that. I used to have a girlfriend who was into that stuff, and it made her crazy."

Catie glanced at her father. He was a very handsome man. He was the best-looking dad in her circle of friends. Nobody had a dad as handsome as Martin William Rezo. When he came to school events, all Catie's friends raved about him. A couple of kids at Marshall who didn't know Catie even thought he was her older brother.

From time to time her dad would toss out anecdotes about his girlfriends, and Catie figured he'd always had plenty of them. If her dad was as good-looking at 18 as he was now, Catie figured he was probably the best-looking guy in high school too. It bothered her a little bit when her father talked about his old girlfriends, but her mom just laughed about it.

Catie followed her mom into the kitchen to help set the table for dinner. Mrs. Rezo was a music teacher at a local college, and she had passed down her love of music to Catie. Like her mom, Catie had a lovely soprano voice, and her mom gave her private vocal lessons. Right now Catie was hoping to sing the lead in a musical at Marshall High.

"I guess Dad was really popular in high school, huh, Mom?" Catie asked.

"You could say that," said her mom. "But I got him. I beat out all those other girls." Her mom smiled. She and Catie's dad had known each other in high school, but they hadn't dated. Her mom went on to college, and her dad got married. After his marriage ended they met at a party and began dating. They were married soon after. "Your father was 'the boy most girls want to date.' " Catie's mom continued. "That's what was written under his senior picture."

"Didn't you ever get jealous?" Catie asked.

Her mom laughed. "I didn't even like him in high school, so I wasn't jealous," she said. "And since he put a ring on my finger, I've trusted him completely."

Soon the Rezo family was sitting down to homemade pizza and french fries. After they were through eating, Catie and Leslie began the ritual of clearing the table and cleaning up the kitchen. That was their job. Either their mom or dad cooked, and they cleaned. Their mom used this free time to practice the piano, while their dad just usually relaxed in front of the TV.

Once the kitchen was presentable again, Catie decided that she should look at her algebra once more. She wasn't feeling entirely ready for the test the next day. She hadn't been doing too well so far in this class, and she didn't want her grade point to suffer because of it.

She set up camp at the kitchen table, spreading out her book and her notes. Once again she went over formulas and practiced sample problems Ms. Bricker had given them in class.

Finally, when her eyes were beginning to glaze over from staring at numbers so long, she decided she had studied as much as she could for the night. As she headed toward her room, the wastebasket caught her eye. She decided to retrieve her chain letter. It would make for a good laugh with her friends the next day. And maybe she'd be able to figure out the writing on the envelope.

It's not as if Catie hadn't received chain letters before. Nearly every time she opened her email, she was bombarded with forwarded messages urging that she pass them on. Some promised good luck if she forwarded them to five friends, and some even claimed that she would receive gift certificates from stores. Although she had yet to find a gift certificate waiting for her in the mailbox.

But Catie knew all those email chain letters were in fun. And she always knew whom they came from. She could see the email address of the sender at the top of each message. But for some reason, not knowing whom this "snail mail" chain letter came from was really bothering her . . .

She dug in the wastebasket and, to her surprise, found the letter and envelope gone. She stuck her head into the living room. "Did you take that chain letter out of the trash?" she asked her dad. "I can't find it in the wastebasket where I threw it."

"Just forget about it, honey," her dad said absently. He was already absorbed in some documentary.

Catie went up to Leslie's room then. "Leslie," she called through the closed door. "Have you seen my chain letter?" Catie could hear the sound effects of a wild computer game. It sounded as if there were some sort of battle going on. Catie opened the door and shouted over the noise, "Leslie, did you see my chain letter in the trash?"

"Huh? What?" Leslie yelled. Catie could see bloody zombies wandering across the computer screen in pursuit of a terrified-looking young woman. A huge cockroach joined the action, and the young woman screamed in terror.

"What kind of garbage is that?" Catie asked, repulsed.

"It's not garbage," Leslie said. "It's a really cool game. Everybody is playing it. This girl has been captured by swamp zombies, and she's trying to get away. She's got an AK-47 stashed, and pretty soon she's gonna blast 'em. The swamp zombies eat humans!"

"Nice," Catie said sarcastically. "So have you seen my chain letter or not?"

"Oh, yeah," Leslie said, not taking her eyes off the screen. "I took it out of the trash and taped it together again. I wanted to show my friends. It's over there on my nightstand."

"Thanks for asking," Catie said to her sister as she walked toward the nightstand. Although Catie and Leslie were five years apart, they usually got along pretty well. But every so often Leslie managed to do something to annoy Catie and make her glad that in their new house they had separate bedrooms.

Catie found the letter, neatly taped together again, and took it to her room. Last year most of Catie's sophomore friends had signed her yearbook, so she thought she might be able to match the handwriting on the envelope.

Kristen Trotter was Catie's best friend, and the girls often played harmless little tricks on each other just for fun. She might have sent the chain letter. But the writing was wildly different from Kristen's. It surely wasn't Todd's writing either. Not that she ever thought for a minute that Todd would do something so strange.

Catie checked the handwriting of everybody who'd signed her yearbook, but she couldn't find a match with the envelope. She decided she would keep the letter, so she stuffed it in her purse. Maybe later on she'd want to check the handwriting with another sample. And she thought Kristen might recognize the writing.

That night Catie went to bed dreaming of equations, swamp zombies, and chain letters.

***

The next day Catie dreaded going to Ms. Bricker's class. She was nervous about the test. Even though she felt she had studied a lot, she was afraid it wasn't enough for the tough teacher's algebra exam.

However, once she got through three problems with ease, she began feeling more confident. As she finished the test with three minutes to spare, she sat back in her chair and took a deep breath.

When the bell rang, Catie found herself walking out of the room beside Ruben Martinez. Once Ruben had asked Catie to a movie, but she was interested in Todd, so she turned him down. She felt bad about it though. Ruben had seemed really disappointed. Catie knew his parents were divorcing, so he had a lot to deal with. She was sorry she had added to his sadness. Ruben was a good-looking guy, but he was shy and not nearly as popular as Todd.

"How do you think you did?" Catie asked Ruben as they crossed the threshold into the outdoor corridor.

"I think I made it," Ruben replied. "It wasn't as hard as I thought it was going to be."

"I guess we both made it today, Ruben," Catie said, smiling. He returned her smile and said, "Yeah! Whew!"

Todd was standing at his locker, and Catie stopped, letting Ruben walk by.

"How was the test?" Todd asked her.

"I think all my studying finally paid off," Catie said.

"Great," Todd said, smiling. "I knew you could do it." Catie really did like Todd. Some people thought he was a little bit arrogant, but Catie figured that he was good-looking, smart, and a great athlete, so he had reason to be satisfied with himself.

"Want to stop for pizza after school?" Todd asked Catie. "I don't really want to eat what the cafeteria is trying to pass off as steak today."

"Sure," Catie said, her heart pounding a little. She was still afraid to believe that Todd liked her more than just as a good friend.

***

After school, as Catie and Todd were having pizza in the popular hangout for Marshall students, Catie pulled the chain letter out of her purse. Several friends and other kids from school paused in their own conversations to listen in as Catie told Todd about it.

"You shouldn't have broken the chain," Todd said.

"What?" Catie asked, surprised. "Todd, it was a stupid chain letter. You know how crazy those are!"

"So what's the harm in playing along with the gag?" Todd asked. "Maybe there's nothing to the chain letter's curse, but what if there is?"

Kristen and two other girls in the next booth laughed.

"Todd, you *seriously* think breaking a chain letter brings bad luck?" Kristen asked.

Todd wiped pizza sauce off the side of his mouth and said, "Why take chances? I read my horoscope every day. If it says today is a day I'm accident-prone, then I watch my step a little more, okay? Look, Catie, maybe there's nothing to it, but better safe than sorry."

"But, Todd, it's so ridiculous," Catie insisted.

Todd didn't smile. "You have your opinions, and I have mine. Don't tell me that if a black cat crosses your path, you don't feel weird. You're never a little rattled on Friday the 13th, right? Catie, we're *all* a little bit superstitious," he said.

Some of the other students joined in the discussion, some on Catie's side and some on Todd's. But Catie stated firmly that she was breaking the chain letter and wasn't one bit sorry.

***

Catie managed to forget all about the chain letter for several days. The deadline the letter warned her to observe came and went. Consequences of breaking the chain were the furthest thing from her mind until one day as she walked out of her American literature class. Heading down the outdoor corridor for the cafeteria, she reached into her purse for her wallet. Immediately, she threw the purse down with a scream.

A huge tarantula was crawling between her wallet and her compact. The hairy creature had brushed against her hand . . .

2 Catie's purse hit the sidewalk, spilling out all its contents. A girl who was right behind Catie rushed over. "What's the matter?" she asked. "Are you okay?"

"Oh, my gosh," Catie screamed. "There's a tarantula in my purse! Get it out, please!"

The girl cautiously knelt by the purse. She poked around inside with a stick. When she felt nothing, she carefully peered inside. "I don't see it anymore," she said. "It probably fell out with everything else and crawled off into the hedge." She began gathering Catie's stuff.

"Are you sure it's gone?" Catie asked, still trembling. The rational part of Catie knew that tarantulas usually did no harm, but the rest of her was completely freaked out any time she saw one—especially by surprise.

"Yeah, it's not in here," the girl answered. Catie tentatively joined the girl in searching the purse. Then they put everything back.

"How do you think it got in there?" Catie asked, shuddering.

The girl said, "This desert is full of tarantulas. It probably crawled in your purse during the spirit assembly this morning when we were all sitting on the bleachers. There's a lot of brush there."

"Yeah, you're right," Catie said. The vacant fields behind Marshall High led into brushy fields and then the foothills, which were teeming with wild things. "Oh, thanks so much for helping me. You came along at just the right time, and I don't even know your name. I'm so embarrassed."

"That's okay. I just started here about a week ago. I'm Marty Jordan," the girl said. "I just transferred to Marshall."

"I'm Catie Rezo," Catie said.

"I know," Marty said. "I saw you sing your solo with the swing choir last Friday. You were good."

"What year are you?" Catie asked.

"Senior," said Marty.

"Well, it's nice to meet you, and thanks

again," Catie said.

Catie continued on to the cafeteria. She usually ate with Kristen or Todd. She got a tray and filled it with today's specialty— spaghetti and meatballs and garlic bread. Then she joined Todd and his friends.

"Hey, what kept you?" Todd asked.

"You wouldn't believe what just happened," Catie said. "A big, hairy tarantula crawled into my purse, and when I reached in to grab my wallet, I touched it! It was so gross! It must've crawled in when we had the assembly."

Todd was silent for a moment while he chewed a mouthful of pasta. Then he said, "Well, what did I say?"

"What do you mean?" Catie asked.

"The chain letter. You just ignored it and . . ." Todd let the sentence drift.

"Oh, Todd!" Catie cried indignantly. "And now the tarantula crawled into my purse, right? Come on! Like whatever freak sent me that chain letter commanded the tarantula to crawl into my purse. Gimme a break!"

"Okay, okay," Todd said, backing off. "Calm down. It's just pretty weird that something like that happens now. Call it coincidence, Catie, but yesterday was the last day you had to send out the other chain letters, right?"

Catie thought for a moment. "Well, yeah, but—" She stared at Todd.

"I rest my case," Todd said. He speared some spaghetti on his fork and ate it.

Catie remembered what Leslie had said about Todd being weird. Maybe he *had* sent the chain letter, Catie thought. He might have gotten a friend to address the envelope so she wouldn't recognize his handwriting. Maybe he was enjoying toying with Catie like this. Maybe he was some power freak who got a kick out of it.

No, Catie told herself, that was ridiculous.

"You know, Catie," Todd said, his face very serious. "I'm into stuff like this, the paranormal and all that. My mom used to consult fortune-tellers all the time when she was young. She was engaged to some guy, and the fortune-teller told her to call off the marriage, so she did."

"That was dumb," Catie said.

"Actually, it turned out that the fortune-teller was right," countered Todd. "The guy turned out to be a criminal. He's up in the state prison yet for murder."

Catie stared at Todd. "Are you serious?" she asked him.

"Yeah," said Todd. "I'd tell you to go back and follow the instructions in that chain letter now, but you waited too long. Whatever consequences there are have been set in motion. You can't do anything now but hope for the best."

"Todd, you're freaking me out," Catie said.

"Sorry," he said with a smile that made Catie blush. "I just care about you."

Catie concentrated on her afternoon classes, especially American history. She had a shot at getting an A in history, and that would bring up her grade point average this semester. Her first couple years of high school she did okay in her classes, but she didn't try as hard as she could've. She just didn't take her studies seriously. Now, as a junior, she was beginning to understand that her grades would play an important role in what she did after high school. She was beginning to see the light at the end of the tunnel, and she didn't want any regrets.

***

Catie's family lived about two miles from Marshall High. Occasionally Catie took the bus, mostly if it was raining, but in good weather she walked to and from school. It was a nice walk down a brushy path to the new development where the Rezos lived—Juniper Hills. Catie often saw rabbits, their white tails bobbing as they ran, roadrunners, and all kinds of birds as she walked. She thought it was relaxing.

Catie's parents had sold their old house nearer town last year and bought one of the beautiful new homes in Juniper Hills. The houses were expensive, but her dad was doing so well now that he said his family deserved the best. Catie's mom was really thrilled to be living in a nice new house with a yard big enough for her gardening hobby, especially her prize roses, which were blooming beautifully. Catie and Leslie loved the new home too. They'd had to share a room in their old house, but in the new one, they each got their own big bedroom.

Catie started her walk home after practicing with the swing choir. She noticed a red-tailed hawk swooping down into the brush. She was still watching it when she thought she heard a dog barking. She turned to see a large dog on the path behind her, several hundred yards away. It was a big, tawny dog, and it was coming toward her on the run, barking and snarling ferociously.

In all the time Catie had walked this path she had never seen this dog. Sometimes other walkers would pass by with dogs on leashes, but no dog had ever menaced her before. This dog was alone with no collar and no leash.

Catie started to become hysterical. What if it attacks me? she thought. She had read somewhere that if you run from a dog, it will pursue you and bring you down. There is no way I can outrun this big dog, she thought.

Quickly, she tried to think of what she had read you were supposed to do. Suddenly, she remembered. She turned and faced the dog. She looked around desperately and snatched up a small stick that had broken off a greasewood bush.

As the dog came closer, Catie yelled, "Go away! Go home!" At the same time she waved the stick and struck the ground with it, making a snapping sound.

The dog paused. It snarled, and its eyes were wild with fury. Saliva dripped from its red mouth. Catie could see the jagged white teeth. She was nearly frozen with fear. But she kept yelling and snapping the stick while the dog wheeled.

"Get back!" Catie screamed. "Go away!"

Catie continued to face the dog. She yelled and waved the stick. She kept trying to scare it by striking the ground with the stick. The dog just snarled and made little steps into Catie's space as if testing the water.

Then somebody whistled. The dog's ears perked up. He turned and bounded back along the way he had come. He leaped over the brushy pathway, through the yellow mustard blowing in the wind.

Catie broke into a cold sweat. She was still trembling when a figure in a striped tank top and jeans appeared. Catie recognized her. It was Marty Jordan.

"Is that your dog?" Catie asked. "Oh, I was terrified. He was acting like he wanted to tear me apart!"

"No, it's a neighbor dog," replied Marty. "But when you whistle, he goes home. I guess he's trained that way. He got out of his fence. Must've been a hole in it, I guess. He's a really dangerous dog. I'm so scared of him that I asked the neighbor what to do if he gets out and comes in our yard. The guy said just to whistle, and he'll break off any fight."

"Thank God you came along," Catie said. "I was so scared, I almost died!"

Marty smiled. "I'll tell the guy who owns Bruno what he did. Bruno—that's the dog's name. Hopefully the owner will build a better fence," she said.

"Wow, that's the second time today you've come to my rescue," Catie said to Marty. "First you help me pick up my purse, and now this. I guess we were meant to be friends!" After a pause, Catie added, "Do you think that dog will come back?"

"I don't think so," Marty said. "But I'll walk with you if you want."

"Oh, do you live in Juniper Hills too?" Catie asked.

"No, but my mom works there," said Marty. "She cleans houses for some rich people. I'm meeting her after she finishes the last house. Then we'll catch a bus and go downtown and see a movie."

"What does your dad do?" Catie asked.

"Oh, he hasn't been around for a long, long time," Marty replied. "I don't remember ever seeing him, in fact. He left Mom before I was born."

"Oh, I'm sorry," Catie said. She felt bad that this nice girl who had helped her twice already apparently didn't have a very good life. She thought it must be very hard to grow up without a dad.

Marty shrugged though and said, "Well, stuff happens, right? What can you do about it? How about your family? Does your mom work?"

"Yeah, she's a music teacher. She taught me to love music. And my dad is an electrical contractor," Catie said. She felt a little self-conscious, like maybe her words were sounding like bragging, though that was the last thing she intended. "So, Marty, do you like Marshall so far?"

"Yeah. It has better teachers, and the computer lab is pretty cool," Marty said. "I've gone to lots of high schools. Marshall is better than most of them. I hope it's the last one before I graduate. I'm almost 19, you know. Most of the seniors are 17 and 18. I've missed out on a lot of school while Mom and I moved all over the country."

When the Juniper Hills housing development loomed, Catie turned to Marty and smiled. "Thanks again for being so nice. I hope we see a lot of each other at school," she said.

"I hope nothing else bad happens to you today," Marty said. "I think you've had your share."

Catie blurted out the whole story of the chain letter then. "It's like the curse of not doing what the chain letter told me to do is coming true," she said, summing it up. "I don't really believe that, but sometimes I wonder."

Marty shrugged. "Yeah, it does make

you wonder, huh?" she said.

The girls separated then, and Catie walked down the street toward home.

***

Todd came over that evening to help Catie with a history project. After they had worked on the project for a while, they sat on the couch and watched TV for a few minutes. Todd put his arm around Catie's shoulders. A few minutes later, Catie's dad came home. He looked at Catie and Todd as he walked into the living room. He didn't say anything, but Catie could see the disapproval in his eyes.

3 Catie figured that after Todd went home, her father would once again deliver the standard "don't-get-too-deeply-involved-with-any-one-boy-at-your-age" speech.

Todd left around 8:00. Catie was doing research on her computer when her dad ambled into her room. "How's the research coming, sweetheart?" he asked.

"Okay, Dad," she said. "I'm researching the League of Nations, which was about a hundred years ago. Ancient history!" Catie said, making a face.

"Not quite right," her dad said. "The League of Nations started right after World War I, around 1919. And when you say ancient history, it brings to mind the Greeks and the Romans. Uh . . . by the way, Catie, Todd is a nice young man. You know, I like him. He's a great football player too. I remember that incredible pass he caught last season. But, uh, he's not getting too pushy, is he?"

Catie looked up from the computer screen. *This* is what Dad came in to talk about, she thought. "No, Dad, everything is cool," she told him.

"Catie, I'm an expert on teenage boys," her dad said. "I guess that's because I was one, and the memory is real fresh. I *was* a pain in the neck when I was Todd's age, and I came on real strong to pretty girls. You know I was already married when I was only 18, which was the stupidest thing I ever did. Luckily, there were no kids and the marriage was ended before it ruined both our lives. But I *know* what Todd is feeling. He's a red-blooded, healthy young male. I just don't want you getting involved with a guy at your age. Just keep it on a friendship level . . ."

Catie had always known about her father's disastrous early marriage. Catie's parents kept no dark secrets from their children. Catie knew about Alicia Monahan, who was nicknamed "Buttons" because of her bright, doll-like eyes. She and Catie's dad had eloped and gotten married to the shock of both sets of parents. Her dad always said they went together like fire and ice. The marriage lasted just five months. He always said he "grew up" during that time. So after the marriage was over and he saw Catie's mom again, though he was still young, he was finally mature enough to know what he wanted.

"I know what you're saying, Dad. But Todd and I aren't serious," Catie said.

"Well, good. Just keep a good head on your shoulders," her dad said.

"Yeah, sure, Dad," Catie said. She went back to the computer, and her dad returned to the living room. She didn't really enjoy listening to his lectures. Her dad preached a lot more than her mom. But her mom taught as much, if not more, just by how she acted—calm, steady, generous, and thoughtful.

Anyway, Catie thought, she probably wasn't in love with Todd. She liked him right now more than she liked any other guy she knew, but she was only 16. She was sure she'd meet a lot more people.

***

Early the next morning Catie heard an angry shout that woke her up. It sounded like her dad. He had to get up early in the morning, before the sun came up. He had been working on a project 70 miles away and needed to get an early start.

Catie pulled on a robe and hurried downstairs. "Dad! What's wrong?" she asked, pushing open the front door. Her dad always parked his truck in the driveway because there was no room in the garage. Catie's mom's car and the old Oldsmobile her dad was restoring took up all the inside space.

Catie's dad was standing in the driveway by his truck. "All four tires have been slashed," he fumed. "Can you believe that? This is the best neighborhood we've ever lived in, and look what's happened. My new truck has been vandalized! What is this world coming to?"

Catie stood there staring at the flat tires. She could tell by the lacerations that they had been savagely ripped with some sharp object. She felt numb. In her whole life, nothing like this had ever happened to her family. The worst thing that had happened before this was a pumpkin smashed on their driveway on Halloween.

Catie thought about the chain letter again. She didn't want to make the connection, but there it was, nagging at her.

Catie's mom and sister had also been awakened by the shouts. They ran downstairs and stared at the truck.

"Oh, Dad, you don't think it is because of that chain letter I ignored, do you?" Catie asked in a shaky voice.

He clamped his hand to his head in frustration. "Good grief, Catie, haven't I got enough trouble without you babbling nonsense? Some little hoodlums must have come down our street last night and slashed the tires on all vehicles parked outside!" he said.

Catie nodded. It made sense what her dad was saying. She often heard about vandals targeting a neighborhood and breaking windows, slashing tires, maybe snapping off the antennas on the cars.

But when Catie looked around, she noticed the van next door was also parked in the driveway, and it was unhurt. So were the sedan across the street and the motor home.

Why was just the Rezo pickup vandalized?

Catie's mom told her husband to take her car to work. She said she'd call a coworker to pick her up to take her to the college. As her dad drove off, Catie was tired but knew she wouldn't be able to go back to sleep. Instead, she lay on the couch and wondered what was going on in her life.

She decided to take the bus to school this morning. She didn't feel like taking that long walk, especially after the tire slashing and the vicious dog yesterday. When Catie got on the school bus, Triana Worth, another junior, hailed her. "Hi, Catie, how's it going?"

"Not so good," Catie said. "Somebody slashed the tires on my dad's truck this morning. Dad was really freaked. And he was late for work and everything."

"Wow!" Triana said. "And you live in that great new neighborhood too. Did you make some enemies or what?"

"Everybody in the neighborhood has been nice and friendly," Catie said. "We can't figure it out. The scary part is that our truck was the only one that was hit."

Kristen came on the bus then and sat

beside Catie. Catie told her friend all that had happened. "Maybe I was wrong in throwing away that chain letter and not going along with it, huh, Kristen?" she said.

Kristen grimaced. "Catie, no way! This is all some weird coincidence. Everybody with any sense throws away chain letters. They have no power to bring bad luck. They're just annoying."

Triana and Catie were in competition to play the lead role of Jasmine Jefferson in *New Orleans Nights*. It was the biggest musical ever performed at Marshall, and the costumes and props were going to be elaborate. Both girls were dying for the lead role of the Creole beauty, Jasmine.

Suddenly a dark thought crossed Catie's mind. Maybe Triana was somehow behind the bad things that were happening to her. Maybe she thought if she played a string of dirty tricks on Catie, Catie would be so rattled that she'd fail the audition.

Catie knew it was a far-out thought, but Triana *did* want the role pretty badly . . .

Catie remembered Triana being very

vindictive last season when she lost a place on the volleyball team to a more talented player. She kept saying cruel things to the girl about her physical appearance and reduced her to tears several times. Catie wasn't sure, but she suspected that Triana was also behind spreading false rumors about the girl being on drugs. Triana denied she was the one who started the rumor, but she had certainly helped spread it with enthusiasm.

"So, did you guys call the police about the slashed tires?" Kristen asked.

"Yeah," Catie said. "Dad is filing a report today. The police are so busy on the more serious crimes that they can't come right out anymore for vandalism."

"Wow," Triana piped up from the seat behind Catie and Kristen, "with all that's going on in your life, how can you prepare for the audition for *New Orleans Nights*?"

"My mom is helping me a lot," Catie said. "She plays the piano while I rehearse the song I'm doing. She's given me some really good pointers. She teaches music in college, you know."

"That's not fair, is it?" Triana asked in a petulant voice. "The other girls who're trying out are amateurs, and you're being helped by a real music teacher. It's like a professional athlete competing in the Olympics. I don't have a professional musician helping me prepare for the audition."

Catie glanced back at Triana. "You have a really good voice, Triana. When we had the sophomore talent show, you won, remember? You've got perfect pitch," she said.

The bus pulled into the parking lot of Marshall High then, and Catie was grateful. She didn't feel like carrying on any more of this conversation with Triana.

After stopping at her locker, Catie walked to her first class, English. When she entered the room, Ms. Lederman seemed surprised to see her. "Why, Catie, I'm so glad to see you. Somebody told me she had heard you were in a terrible auto accident and were in the hospital," Ms. Lederman said.

"There must have been a mistake," Catie said. "I wasn't in any accident. I don't even drive a car. Who told you that?"

"A young lady said your mother had called the school office and told them about an accident. We were all going to sign a card," Ms. Lederman said.

"My mom never called the school about anything like that," Catie said.

Catie was shaken once again. Somebody had maliciously planted a false rumor just to rattle Catie. Or was it the evil power of the chain letter, rattling events in Catie's universe? Did the chain letter have the power to just make everything go *wrong*?

At lunch Catie told Todd about the false rumor. "I'm to the point that I don't know what I think," Catie wailed. She had little appetite for the tuna casserole before her.

Todd shook his head. "Maybe you should go see somebody who can break spells," he said.

"Are you serious?" Catie asked.

"Sure," said Todd. "There's a woman over in Thompson Grove who does stuff like that. She claims she can break curses and evil spells. My aunt swears by her."

"But, Todd, that is so weird," Catie said.

"Well, all I know is, bad stuff seems to

be happening to you, and maybe this is worth a try. Maybe there's nothing to it, but what harm would it do for you to go over to see Madame Hortense and give her a shot at it?" Todd said. "I could drive you over there after school. Thompson Grove is just about 20 miles west of here."

"Yeah, well, maybe some other time," she said.

Marty came along with her tray then, and Catie invited her to join them. It was the least Catie could do for the new girl when she had come to Catie's rescue twice.

Catie introduced Marty to Todd and brought Marty up to date on what was happening. "Todd thinks I should go to some witch who can break spells," Catie said.

Todd frowned. "She's *not* a witch! She's a psychic healer," he said, obviously irked.

"Well," Marty said, "that might not be a bad idea. My mom always reads her horoscope to see what she should do. Not that it seems to help her any . . ."

Catie thought about her own life. She could remember few really bad incidents. The worst that had happened was when she broke her leg in-line skating when she was 12.

Marty nibbled on her tuna casserole and said, "My whole life has been sorta cursed. If somebody put a chain letter curse on me, I probably wouldn't even notice the difference."

"But you're doing well at Marshall so far, aren't you?" Catie asked. She thought that Marty was such a pretty, nice girl. She deserved a few good breaks.

"Yeah, so far," said Marty. "But Mom and I have bounced all around the country. She was always looking for some good spot for us, but it seemed like she never found it. We even lived out of our car for a while . . . And now she's been busted for stealing jewelry at a place where she works . . ."

Catie was shocked. "What? Stealing jewelry?" she repeated.

"Yeah, but she didn't do it," said Marty. "Those rich ladies misplace their jewelry and then they blame the maid or the cleaning lady."

"That's not right," Catie said. "I'm sure your mom will be cleared."

"Rich people always think the help is

stealing from them," Marty said. "This isn't the first time."

"You need to get a good lawyer," Todd said.

"Yeah, right," Marty said. "Like we can afford that."

Marty excused herself before the bell rang signaling the end of the lunch period. She had to get to P.E. class and change her clothes. Just as Catie and Todd were getting up to dump their trays, Triana walked over. "Catie," she said, "Mr. Baron is scheduling a meeting in the auditorium to prepare for the auditions. I just got word saying we've got to be at the auditorium right after the last class today."

"I wonder why nobody told me," Catie said.

"Because," Triana said coldly, "I guess they expected I'd tell you."

***

When Catie finished her last class, she walked over to the auditorium. But when she got there, there was a note taped to the front door.

"Meeting for *New Orleans Nights* planning, go to Room 117."

Catie was surprised. Room 117 was usually used by the fine arts students to make pottery. It was a cement building filled with kilns for baking clay and paints for glazing. Maybe another activity had pushed Mr. Baron out of the auditorium, Catie thought.

Catie walked down to Room 117. When she knocked on the door, it sprang open. It was dark inside. Apparently she was the first student who had reported to the auditorium and found the note telling her to come here.

"Anybody here?" Catie asked, but she knew there wasn't. The room smelled of paint and clay. Even though it was dark, Catie could see the outline of stuff all over the floor—newspapers, brushes, half empty cans of paint. Catie walked slowly into the room and began looking for the light.

Suddenly Catie saw a figure leap up behind her, a figure that had been hiding in the shadows. The person gave Catie a violent shove into a walk-in closet. Catie was stunned by the attack, and she stumbled headfirst into the closet. Before she could whirl around and escape or even see her attacker, the closet door was slammed shut and locked from the outside. The small closet was plunged into total darkness.

Catie grabbed for the doorknob. She couldn't believe what had happened. "Let me out!" she screamed. She pounded on the inside of the door with both fists. "Let me out!"

But Catie realized with a sickening fear that the cement arts and crafts classrooms were some distance from the main campus of Marshall High, and it was unlikely anyone could hear her scream.

4 Still Catie continued pounding on the door and screaming for help. Surely other students who were planning to audition for *New Orleans Nights* had gone to the auditorium as she did and found the same note directing them here. They would soon be milling around, wondering what was going on.

Or wouldn't there be any other students?

Was the message from Triana a hoax? Was the note on the auditorium door meant just for Catie, to lure her here, to trap her?

Triana! It had to be Triana! Catie did not know how Triana managed to get the tarantula into her purse, or how she had loosed the vicious dog on her. She didn't know how she had slashed the tires of her dad's truck, but she *knew* it was Triana Worth who had lured her here!

"Help!" Catie screamed as loudly as she could. She pounded so hard on the door that she was bruising her knuckles. Somebody *had* to hear her, she thought. There were students left on the campus, and surely one of them was an art student who might wander by in search of some paint or to check on a piece of work. And what about the maintenance people? They surely came around to clean up! But when? How long would Catie have to be imprisoned in the closet?

Catie had not seen who had pushed her. She hadn't even caught a quick glimpse of the person. It had all happened so fast. It had caught her completely by surprise. But she was sure it had to be Triana. She had seemed so angry that morning when Catie mentioned that her mom was helping her prepare for the auditions. And look at all the trouble Triana had made last year for that poor girl who took her spot on the volleyball team. She had made that girl's life miserable for weeks.

Catie smelled something then—an acrid smell.

Smoke!

"Noooo," Catie gasped. She pounded on the door with even more fury. "Help me!"

she screamed until her lungs hurt. What if someone had set the room afire? All those paint palettes and newspapers would quickly become an inferno. And Catie was trapped in the closet!

Catie began kicking at the door as hard as she could. Maybe she could kick a hole in it, she thought. Then she could reach up through the hole and open the door.

But the door was strong, and her kicking only made her toes sore. "Help!" Catie screamed again.

Catie's breath came now in rapid gasps. She thought the classroom would soon be on fire and she was doomed. It didn't seem possible that Triana would do such a thing to her over the lead in a school musical, and yet people were doing horrifying things all the time. The newspapers and television were full of reports of them, only you never thought they'd happen to you.

Catie began to sob as she kicked the locked door and continued to beat her bruised fists on the wood. "Help me!" she screamed.

Catie suddenly froze. Footsteps . . .

There was someone in the room!

"Oh, thank God, thank God," Catie gasped. She yelled, "I'm trapped in here! Oh, please, let me out!"

She could tell that someone was standing at the door of the closet. A key turned in the lock. As the door opened, Catie could see Ms. Bricker standing with the janitor. Ms. Bricker looked angry, which Catie could not understand.

"Someone lured me into this room," Catie babbled. "Then she pushed me into the closet and slammed it after me, and then there was a . . . fire. I smelled smoke," Catie looked around the room. She didn't see anything burning.

"Give me a break," Ms. Bricker snorted. "You sneaked in here to smoke cigarettes, and the door slammed on you. There's a wind out today, and doors are slamming all over the place."

"No! I didn't," Catie cried. "I don't smoke, and I was pushed into this closet!"

"Students are always sneaking around smoking," Ms. Bricker growled. "And I found a lit cigarette on the floor. I had to stamp it out. You probably heard someone coming, and you hid in the closet. Then the wind pushed the door shut."

Catie was stunned. How could Ms. Bricker think such a thing? Catie was not a troublemaker. She'd never even gotten a tardy slip or a detention.

"I was tipped off by another student that you had come in here to smoke, and somehow you got trapped," Ms. Bricker said.

"What student?" Catie demanded. "She's probably the one who pushed me into the closet!"

"Oh, please!" Ms. Bricker snapped. "Look at all the cigarette butts on the floor! You kids are always sneaking in here. And it's dangerous. You could start a fire! For goodness sakes, you could have burned the whole place down."

At that moment Catie noticed her purse lying in the middle of the floor. She must have dropped it when she was pushed so violently. Or else the person who pushed her yanked it from her grasp. She had been so shocked, she couldn't remember. As Catie went to retrieve her purse, Ms. Bricker said, "Just one moment, Catie.

Please spill the contents of your purse on the table there. Let's just see if we find any cigarettes in your purse."

Catie dumped the purse, and her stuff went all over the table. A half empty pack of cigarettes tumbled out with her compact, followed by a matchbook and a lighter.

"Aha," Ms. Bricker said triumphantly.

"I've never seen those things before in my life," Catie cried. "Somebody planted those in my purse while I was stuck in the closet!"

"Please," Ms. Bricker said. "No more excuses! Because you're a good student with no disciplinary problems on your record, we'll just forget this little escapade. Plus, it's Friday. You've already made me late getting home. I don't want to stay longer filling out paperwork. But be warned, young lady. If you are *ever* caught smoking on campus again, you will be suspended from school. I understand that you are competing for the lead in the school musical. If you mess up, you can just kiss that opportunity good-bye! No extracurricular activities for students with a suspension on their records!"

Catie took her purse and hurried from the room. She was mortified. And the more she thought about what had happened to her, the more it had the earmarks of something Triana would do. Somebody getting something Triana wanted was just too much for her to bear. She was determined to destroy Catie's chances of having the lead in the musical even before the auditions.

Catie walked from the school in the dusk, wondering how she'd get home. The buses weren't taking students from Marshall High anymore at this hour. Catie didn't want to walk that lonely, brushy trail, and she hated to call her parents to come get her. But she figured she'd probably have to.

But then a broken-down old pickup rattled to a stop where Catie was walking toward the pay phone that stood outside the gymnasium. "Hey, you look sorta lost," a boy's voice called to her.

Catie turned to see Ruben from her math and history classes. He was tall and thin with thick dark hair. Though he was pretty shy, he had very beautiful, expressive dark eyes.

"Oh, I was just trying to figure out how to

get home. I missed my bus," Catie explained.

"I'll drive you home," Ruben offered immediately.

"Are you sure? It isn't too much out of your way? I'd hate to put you out, Ruben," Catie said, remembering how she had rebuffed his attempts to date her.

"No, it's no problem," Ruben said. He leaned over and unlocked the door on the passenger side. "Just get in. I hope you don't mind riding in such an old wreck, but it gets me from here to there, and I guess that's all that matters."

Catie climbed in gratefully. "This is so nice of you. I was really stuck." The ceiling upholstery hung in billows on Catie's head, and the stuffing was oozing out of the seat.

"I'm sorry this truck is such a mess," Ruben apologized.

"Oh, Ruben, I'm just so thankful for a ride home. I would have gladly climbed onto a garbage truck!" Catie said.

Ruben laughed a little. She had never seen him laugh before. Catie thought he looked cute when he laughed. But then he

quickly turned serious again. "So how did
you miss your bus?" he asked. "Did you
have to stay late for a class or something?"

Catie explained what had happened
and Ms. Bricker's accusations.

Ruben looked surprised. "Why would
someone set you up like that?" he asked.

"I don't know why. I walked into the
room expecting that the musical group
was meeting there. The next thing I knew,
somebody shoved me into a closet and
slammed and locked the door," she said.

On the drive to Juniper Hills, Catie told
Ruben about the chain letter and all the
awful things that had happened to her
after she ignored it. "I don't know if
there's a curse on me because I didn't do
what the chain letter said or not," Catie
groaned.

"That's superstition," Ruben said.
"Somebody is messing with your mind. A
lot of people believe in stuff like chain
letters and tarot cards, but it's all just
superstition."

Catie felt better that someone else felt
as she did—or thought she did, anyway.

"It's so nice of you to go out of your

way to bring me home like this. I really appreciate it," Catie said as they neared her home.

"It's okay. It's a pleasure," Ruben said with a shy grin. He pulled into Catie's driveway and stopped. "Have a good weekend," he said, smiling shyly. His idling engine sounded like a thrashing machine, but the old truck had gotten Catie safely home.

Once at the door, Catie stopped and waved at Ruben as he drove off.

"You're so late," Catie's mom said when Catie walked in. Her mom's eyes were wide and fearful. "With that tire slashing thing happening to your dad's truck, I was just so worried when you didn't come home on time. I called the school, but the secretary said all the students were gone except for the football team. I was about ready to call the police!"

5 "I'm sorry, Mom," said Catie. "I would've called if I could've. Somebody tricked me into going into an empty classroom way at the edge of the campus and then pushed me into a closet. Then whoever it was slammed the door shut and locked it. I was trapped in there for almost an hour. Oh, Mom, it was horrible!" Just recounting the incident made her voice tremble.

"Catie!" her mom gasped. "Who would do such a horrible thing?"

"I don't know. I've got some suspicions, but I don't have any proof," Catie said.

"Did you tell the teachers what happened? It's a crime to do that to somebody," her mom said indignantly. "I don't even care if it was some sick prank. That's a crime!"

"Ms. Bricker didn't even believe me when I told her what happened. There was a lit cigarette on the floor when she walked in. She thinks I hid in the closet to smoke cigarettes and the door slammed on me from a gust of wind. Oh, Mom, somebody at school has been spreading lies about me, that I sneak around smoking and stuff. Somebody even planted a pack of cigarettes in my purse! It's like there's a horrible conspiracy at school to ruin me!" Catie wailed.

"But, Catie, why would somebody be doing all of this to you? You've never had any trouble before. You've got so many friends, and you've never mentioned any enemies," her mom said.

"Well, I'm competing with Triana Worth for the lead in our school musical. Maybe she's behind it all," said Catie. "She wants the lead really badly. Maybe she's trying to give me a nervous breakdown so I don't even try out for the role."

"You think Triana would be evil enough to do something like that?" her mom asked. "She's not one of my favorite people, but I never dreamed she was vicious!"

"Oh, Mom, *I don't know*!" Catie said. "Maybe all this has nothing to do with Triana. Maybe . . . maybe . . ." Catie's voice faltered. She was almost ready to believe that there was some unnatural evil force launched against her.

"What, Catie? What are you trying to say?" her mom demanded.

"The chain letter . . . maybe when I didn't keep it going I brought this all on myself. I mean, Todd thinks that's what's going on, and maybe he's right. This new girl who's been really nice to me, Marty Jordan, she thinks it could be the chain letter too . . ." Catie said.

"Oh, Catie, that's not possible," her mom said. "You know it isn't. Some sick person is doing this to you, somebody with a twisted sense of humor. This awful person probably knows about the chain letter and is playing on your superstition for this horrible game."

"Yeah," Catie said. Her mind swiftly evaluated her friends at Marshall High. Of course it wouldn't be Kristen, her best friend. Kristen and Catie played silly little pranks on each other, but Kristen would never be involved in slashing tires and sending vicious dogs after Catie. And then there was Todd. He had all these weird hobbies concerning UFOs and fortune-tellers, but Catie didn't think Todd would ever do anything to harm or frighten her.

So Triana was left as the likely suspect. She was the one who had directed Catie to the phony meeting in the art room. She had a strong motive. She had hurt people before when they got something she wanted . . .

"Catie," her mom said, "you have to be really careful. The person doing these things could be dangerous."

"I'll be careful, Mom," Catie said. "But one good thing came out of this anyway. I got to know Ruben Martinez a little more. He was nice enough to drive me home today. I always kind of thought of him as just a shy nobody, but he really is nice."

***

Saturday mornings Catie enjoyed sleeping in and lounging around the house. This particular morning, Leslie was still at a friend's slumber party, so Catie did not have to worry about her sister jumping on her bed and begging her to play a game with her. Catie awoke at

10:00, pulled on her robe, and headed downstairs for some freshly squeezed orange juice. As she was grabbing the pitcher out of the refrigerator, she heard her mother scream. It was coming from the backyard. An icy chill went up Catie's spine as she ran outside to where her mom was standing in her rose garden.

Catie's mom grew many beautiful flowers, but the roses were her pride and joy. Catie had never seen roses in so many vibrant colors.

But now her mom stood before her garden and stared in horror at the ruin. The roses had been slashed with a weed cutter, and some noxious substance had been poured over the remaining roots. Catie's mom looked devastated as she surveyed the garden she had so lovingly and carefully tended.

"Who would do such a thing?" her mom wept. "My beautiful roses! Who would cut them all down and pour poison in my garden? It's so senseless!"

Catie's dad hurried outside, his face disfigured with anger. He knelt on the ground near the roses and sniffed the fouled soil. "Smells like a petroleum product," he said. "Looks like they cut down everything in sight and then poured kerosene or something on the soil. Like they wanted to destroy the soil itself!" Then he went into a tirade that included a few choice words Catie was surprised her dad even knew. He was really shaken. She had never seen her father so upset.

"I don't understand it," her mom wept softly. "Who would want to destroy my lovely roses? Everybody on the street enjoyed them. People who walked would always stop to look at them . . ."

Catie felt as if she might pass out. It was all piling up in a horrible way. The tarantula in her purse, the vicious dog, being trapped in the closet, her dad's slashed tires, the lies against her, and now this. Her mom was sobbing over her dead roses, and her dad was cursing up a blue streak.

It was all too much.

It was as if there really were a curse on the Rezo family, one designed to harass and torment them.

But why?

Catie rushed into the house and called Todd. She was trembling and crying as she hit the buttons on the phone. "Todd, are you busy?" she asked him when he answered.

"Nope, just shooting baskets, baby," Todd said. "What's up?"

"Could you drive me to Thompson Grove right now to see that woman you told me about?" Catie asked desperately. She couldn't take this anymore. She had to do something.

"Yeah, sure," Todd said. "Just hang on, Catie. I'll be there in ten minutes."

Catie ran upstairs, quickly changed into clothes, and was at the curb when Todd pulled up in his old Impala. Catie wasn't sure that she wasn't being foolish, but she felt she had to do it.

"You know, Todd, yesterday afternoon somebody pushed me into the closet in the art room," Catie told him as they drove off. "I was locked in there for almost an hour. I smelled smoke, and I was frantic. I was scared to death!"

"No kidding?" Todd asked. "That's crazy!"

"And this morning somebody totally destroyed Mom's beautiful rose garden," Catie continued. "They slashed all the roses to pieces sometime last night and then poured kerosene or something on the soil. It's just too horrible . . ." Catie said.

Todd shook his head. "You've got big-time problems, sweetie. Maybe Madame Hortense can help you out."

Catie thought Todd was being extra nice to her. Butterflies flew in her stomach as she wondered if it was because he really did like her for more than just someone to go out with once in a while . . .

Then she began to feel foolish as they drew closer to Thompson Grove. She thought maybe she shouldn't be consulting a psychic healer. Maybe she should be confronting Triana Worth. But deep in her heart, she could not believe that Triana could do something so horrifying—all because of a stupid lead in a school musical.

"I don't know if I believe in stuff like this, Todd," Catie said. "I'm just so desperate."

Todd glanced over at Catie and smiled. "This is gonna be pretty exciting. I always wondered how this sort of thing worked. My aunt has been telling me about Madame Hortense for years, but I've never seen the lady in action. My aunt swears she's talked to the dead with the help of Madame Hortense. This will be so cool." His voice throbbed with excitement.

A terrible thought crossed Catie's mind then. Todd seemed so excited and happy about all this. Could he have engineered the whole series of events just to get a psychic experience? Was he that off-the-wall?

"Todd, I'm not even sure this trip is such a good idea," Catie said with a sudden change of heart. "What if a real person is doing this to me, and it's not a spell or anything?"

"Don't bail on me now, baby," Todd said. "Not when we're almost there. Go with the program, Catie. Believe me, you're in for a real trip. What's been happening to you isn't natural. Dark spirits are running wild in your world."

A rickety sign by the side of the road

proclaimed "Thompson Grove."

"But, Todd," Catie argued. "It seems like whoever is doing all this to me and my family hates us!"

"Once you cross a chain letter, you let loose a bad karma, that's all," Todd explained. "See, there are these dark forces out there, and when you get them going against you, you are in major trouble. The bad stuff sorta converges on you. All these bad things are out there circling. When you mess up, they just zero in on you."

Catie looked uneasily at Todd. But he smiled. Catie couldn't help thinking that even though he was kind of weird, he was so cute.

"That's why it's good that you're going to see Madame Hortense," Todd continued. "She'll break the bad-luck cycle."

Catie's head was spinning. She didn't know what to believe. And she began to seriously wonder if Todd and his crazy fascination with the weird *was* behind all of her troubles. Maybe he wrote the chain letter knowing she would break the chain.

Then he planned all those pranks just so they'd end up with Madame Hortense.

"Todd, you didn't send me that chain letter, did you?" Catie asked as they drove through Thompson Grove to the outskirts where Madame Hortense lived.

"Me? Are you joking?" Todd asked. "I wouldn't send anybody a chain letter. I wouldn't want it to backfire on me."

"But you seem so thrilled to be going there," Catie said. "I just don't understand."

"I'm just interested in this stuff, Catie," Todd defended. "There's no crime in that. The person who sent you the chain letter is probably someone you don't even know. Some freshman who found your name and address in the school directory. Or maybe a neighbor. Maybe even the little old lady in the corner bakery."

At the edge of Thompson Grove stood a large Victorian house that looked like the perfect setting for a Halloween haunted house. A hand-painted sign out front read:

Madame Hortense
Psychic consulting
and healing.
Gifted clairvoyant,
auras, spells, crystals.

Catie shivered. She imagined herself having to walk through cobwebs with hordes of spiders waiting to jump on her head. But she left the Impala and followed Todd up the crumbling flagstone walk to the green front door. Weeping willow trees lined the walk, adding to the gloomy appearance of the place.

Catie felt like turning around and running back to the car.

Todd sensed Catie's nervousness and put his arm around her. "Take it easy, babe. You're doing the right thing here. You'll get all this bad stuff out of your life."

Todd knocked on the door, and soon a rather attractive middle-aged woman appeared. She had long black hair and wore a light green silk dress, topped by a fringed green shawl. Catie was sort of expecting someone in black with a peaked witch's hat.

"Madame Hortense," Todd said, "this is my friend, Catie Rezo. She's been having a lot of trouble since she broke a chain letter. We're hoping maybe you can help her."

Madame Hortense smiled at Todd. "Todd, thank you for calling. It is so good to see you. Give your Aunt Lacey my very best wishes. Tell her our seánces will be starting again next month." Then she turned to Catie. "Come along, Catie," she said, holding out a long, bony hand. "We will see what we can do."

Madame Hortense ushered Catie and Todd into a small room through a sparkling beaded curtain. Catie smelled heavy incense. Candles were burning everywhere, giving the room an eerie glow. Madame Hortense motioned for Catie to sit in a large upholstered chair. Todd sat across from her.

"Tell me the whole story, my dear," Madame Hortense instructed, "from the moment you first received the chain letter."

Reluctantly, Catie related all that had happened. Madame Hortense kept nodding knowingly and saying things like "Classic" and "Of course," as if she had heard all this before.

"So what should I do?" Catie finally asked.

"First I must ask you to trust me completely, my dear," Madame Hortense said in her deep, husky voice. She had piercing, dark eyes that seemed to bore a hole into Catie's mind and study her thoughts. Adding to that, Madame Hortense wore heavy makeup. Her green eye shadow flecked with silver glistened in the flickering candlelight.

Suddenly she was glaring at Catie. "You don't trust me!" she cried.

6 "What?" cried Catie. "What do you mean? I didn't say I didn't trust you." But the truth was, Catie didn't trust the strange woman at all.

"You are full of mistrust. I can sense it," Madame Hortense said scornfully. "Listen to me, and I will give you instructions on how to break the dark spell that has enveloped your life. But I fear your mistrust of me will cause terrible conflict that will make my work impossible."

"Catie," Todd advised. "Just relax and put your trust in Madame Hortense. She's really good at this."

Soft, mystical music played in the room, and the smell of incense seemed stronger.

"There is a charge of $100 for my instructions, my dear," Madame Hortense said. "Surely a very small price to pay to relieve you of this terrible misfortune."

"A hundred dollars?" Catie replied. "That's a lot of money!"

"I take credit cards," Madame Hortense said. "Really, dear, you probably spend more than that during an afternoon shopping spree at the mall."

The whole situation appeared to Catie as a gigantic fraud. She figured Madame Hortense would speak some strange words and light more candles, and it wouldn't make any difference in what was happening in Catie's life. She'd never believed in fortune-telling and spells. Only her distraught state after her mom's roses had been vandalized had led her to a momentary weakness in her judgment. Now she saw it all clearly.

"This is all a big fraud," Catie said.

"Catie!" Todd gasped.

Catie stood up. "I just want to get away from here," she said. "I was all wrong in coming here, Todd. Please, let's go home."

"I knew you didn't trust me," Madame Hortense said bitterly. "Todd, take this girl out of my sight at once. You should never have brought her here. I cannot help her. Nobody can. The spell will remain upon her, darkening her life. She is doomed! *Doomed!*"

"I'm really sorry, Madame Hortense," Todd apologized. "I had no idea Catie would react like this."

"Just get her out of here," Madame Hortense demanded, holding her hand to her head as if she were coming down with a severe headache. "This is so troubling."

When Catie and Todd were outside, Catie said, "I'm sorry, Todd. But surely you could see that it was all a scam, couldn't you?"

"You were really rude in there, Catie," Todd said in a cold voice. "You embarrassed me in front of someone who's a close friend of my favorite aunt. Now Aunt Lacey is going to get a call from Madame Hortense. My aunt will be all mad, and she gives me a hundred bucks for my birthdays and Christmas."

"I told you I was sorry, Todd. I just couldn't go through with it." Catie leaned back in the car and closed her eyes. "I shouldn't have asked you to drive me all this way when I knew deep down it was all stupid!"

"You don't know anything, Catie," Todd snapped. "Maybe you *are* under a spell.

Maybe Madame Hortense could have helped you, but you wouldn't even give her a chance."

"Oh, Todd, when you talk like that, I think you're nuts!" Catie cried, immediately regretting her harsh words once they were out.

A hard look came across Todd's face. "You know something, Catie? You're a pretty ungrateful person. I try to help you, and this is the thanks I get. I can't believe you're so immature. And to think that I really liked you. I thought we were on our way to a serious relationship. But you know what? I hope Triana wins the lead in *New Orleans Nights*. She deserves it more. And she's got a better voice too."

The rest of the ride home was in icy silence. Catie was angry and Todd was bitter. Todd had actually admitted that he really did care about Catie as more than just a friend. But she figured that the admission had come too late.

As Todd pulled up to Catie's house, she jumped from the Impala and ran up the walk, never looking back.

Once inside, she began to cry. Now she had lost her shot at having Todd as her boyfriend too. She had told herself that she wasn't that serious about Todd, but now that she knew it was over, she realized how much she really did like him. The curse—or whatever it was— had done it again. It was chipping away at Catie's life, dismantling everything that mattered.

Catie's mom and dad had left a note saying that they were visiting her dad's cousin. He was in the hospital for a hip operation. Only Leslie, just back from spending the night with her friend, was home.

"Did you have fun at the party?" Catie asked Leslie, though she really didn't care about anything just now.

"Yeah, it was great," Leslie said, putting away her sleeping bag. She looked at Catie. "Why are you crying?" she asked in alarm. "What's the matter?"

"Oh, Leslie," Catie said, "you *saw* what happened to Mom's roses, didn't you? It seems like everything is going wrong. I don't know what to do. Ever since that chain letter came, my life has been horrible."

"But I thought chain letters were just a joke," Leslie said. "I didn't think they really worked or anything. I got one like that last year, and I sent the others out like they told me to do. But I thought it was just a joke—like throwing salt over your shoulder and stuff like that. I didn't think they could do bad things." Leslie's voice began to shake.

"Leslie," Catie said, shocked at her little sister's tears. "Chain letters *don't* work. For a little while I was stupid enough to think they do, but something else is happening. Somebody who hates me and wants to hurt me just used the chain letter to start all this awful harassment. Leslie, don't cry."

But the tears streamed in a torrent from Leslie's eyes. "Catie . . ." she sobbed.

"Oh, Leslie," Catie said, putting her arms around her sister and hugging her. "It's not *that* bad. Don't cry. We'll get to the bottom of this and find the creep who sent the chain letter and started all this trouble."

"I . . . I . . ." Leslie tried to speak but the words caught in her throat. Her words drowned in sobs.

"Leslie," Catie pleaded, looking at her little sister, "what's the matter?"

"I—I did it," Leslie cried. "I sent you the chain letter. It was a joke. Elise sent me a chain letter last year, and it was fun. So Paula and I got this idea to send you one just to see what happened. I thought it'd be cool 'cause mine was fun. So we typed the letter. Then Paula wrote on the envelope so you wouldn't recognize my handwriting. We made up the poem and everything. But it was a joke. I didn't think it would hurt you. It was . . . just . . . a . . . joke . . ."

Catie was stunned. If Leslie sent the chain letter, then what was going on? If an enemy was not behind this, had Leslie unknowingly loosed some supernatural horror?

"I b—bet you h—hate me," Leslie wept.

"No, I don't hate you. It was just a dumb stunt," Catie said.

"It's my fault that Daddy's tires were slashed and Mom's roses were all killed.

It's all my fault that something bad is after us," Leslie sobbed again.

Catie grabbed Leslie again and hugged her. "No, it's not your fault. The chain letter has nothing to do with the bad things that are happening around here. Nothing!"

"Nooo," Leslie wailed, "it's all my fault. I made the evil forces come down on us, like the swamp ghouls in my computer game."

"Leslie, that's stupid," Catie said. "There's a girl at school who wants the lead in the school musical, and she thinks I'm going to beat her out of it. I think she's playing all these mean tricks on us to try to mess up my head so I screw up the audition."

"Don't tell Mom and Dad that I sent the chain letter, please, please, Catie," Leslie said. "Dad wouldn't let me use the computer anymore, and I'd be grounded for a hundred years!"

"I won't tell them," Catie promised.

***

At school on Monday, Catie decided to confront Triana and find out once and for

all if she was behind the problems the
Rezo family was having. Catie didn't
expect Triana to admit anything, but at
least Catie could see if she *looked* guilty
when she brought up the subject.

"Hi, Triana," Catie said when Triana
appeared at the front entrance to Marshall
High. "Remember on Friday when you
told me Mr. Baron was having a meeting
for students who wanted to be in *New
Orleans Nights*? Well, I went to the
auditorium, and there was a note telling
us that the meeting was over in Room 117.
I went there, and something really awful
happened. What's up with that? Why did
you steer me wrong?"

Triana's jaw dropped. "*I* didn't steer
anybody wrong. Some girl came up to me
after class and said, 'Hey, you and Catie
are trying out for *New Orleans Nights*,
aren't you? There's a meeting in the
auditorium for you guys. You better tell
Catie.' So I just told you what she told
me," Triana said.

"Who was the girl?" Catie asked.

"I didn't even know her. But she
seemed to know what she was talking

about. What happened to you that was so awful?" Triana asked.

Catie relayed what had happened to her in Room 117.

"Oh, my gosh!" Triana gasped. Catie couldn't tell if she was really shocked or if she was a better actress than Catie had suspected.

"I think there's somebody here at school who's trying to give me a nervous breakdown or something," said Catie.

"That's awful," Triana said. "Who would—"

Catie cut into her sentence in a harsh voice. "How come you didn't go to the auditorium and read the same sign I did and show up at Room 117? Or was that a trap set just for me?"

"I *did* go to the auditorium, a few minutes after the last bell rang," Triana said. "I had to return a book to the library first. I didn't see any sign about Room 117. I waited at the auditorium for about ten minutes. Nobody showed up, so I went home."

"You're sure you can't remember who gave you that message, huh, Triana?"

Catie asked, her voice dripping with sarcasm. "I mean, maybe she was really an alien or something."

Triana looked around wildly at the students arriving for classes. "I'd recognize her if I saw her again. *There*! I see her now. It's that girl with dark hair in the tank top. She's in some of our classes, but I don't know her name."

Catie knew the girl Triana was pointing to. *Marty Jordan*. Catie was getting more suspicious by the minute. Triana was desperately looking for a scapegoat to blame her treachery on. So she pointed to the new girl. Better her than somebody they both knew. If you need to blame somebody, then it's much safer to pick on a stranger . . .

"Hey, Marty," Catie shouted. "Would you come over here for a minute?"

Marty came over and smiled at Catie. "Yeah? What?"

"Did you tell Triana here on Friday that there was a meeting about the school musical in the auditorium?" Catie asked.

Marty looked bewildered. "Huh?" she said. "I don't know what you're talking about. I didn't even know there *was* a school musical."

"Thanks," Catie said. Marty shrugged and walked away. Then Catie turned to Triana. "You told me so I'd go over to the auditorium, find the note you planted, and then go to Room 117. Then you probably threw the note away. You followed me into that dark classroom and ambushed me, Triana. You want to mess me up so I do badly in the audition so you can get the lead. Isn't that true?"

Triana's eyes became very large, and she began to tremble. "Catie Rezo, I cannot believe you are standing there, accusing me of such a terrible thing. How dare you!"

"You know the competition to play Jasmine is just between us," Catie went on. "If you can get me out of the way, then you've got it made. You're behind all the rotten things that've been happening to me and my family. I don't know how you managed to do all those things, but somehow you did. But listen up, Triana. It isn't going to work. I'm going to come through that audition with flying colors, and I'm going to win the part, so all your dirty little tricks are for nothing!"

Boiling hot tears splashed down Triana's cheeks. "I have never been so insulted in my life! I didn't do *anything* to you! That girl was completely lying to you. How can you make those horrible accusations about me?" she cried.

"I remember how you operate, Triana. Last year when Jamie Wilcox beat you out of a spot on the volleyball team, you spread all kinds of false rumors about her just to get even. And now you're trying to undermine me! But it won't work. I don't intend to fall down and play dead!" Catie yelled.

7 "Catie," Triana cried in a shrill, angry voice, "I'm not guilty! I didn't do anything to you! I swear I didn't. I don't even know what you're talking about! Sure, I want to play Jasmine Jefferson in the musical, but I never did anything to mess you up. I didn't!"

Several other students gathered as the girls argued in loud voices. One of the boys yelled, "Cat fight coming down. Gather 'round, boys!"

Todd walked up then. "Why are you picking on Triana?" he asked Catie. "What's your problem?"

Catie didn't answer Todd, and she saw him turn to another guy. "Maybe she's doing all this stuff to herself just to get sympathy," she heard him say.

Catie flushed with embarrassment. It dawned on her then how many of her schoolmates might think just that—that Catie herself was behind her misfortunes.

Locking herself in a closet then screaming foul. Sticking a tarantula into her *own* purse. Messing with her father's tires and her mother's roses . . .

Catie realized then that she was making a fool of herself by having this public altercation with Triana. Especially when she wasn't even sure Triana was the guilty party!

She felt terrible. She was well-liked and respected here at Marshall, and now everything she'd worked so hard to gain was going away. She was acting like a paranoid psycho.

The curse had already cost her her peace of mind, her boyfriend, and now probably all her other friends too!

Kristen appeared from the throng of students just then and grabbed Catie's arm. "Come on, let's get out of here," she said, steering Catie away from the crowd. Catie allowed Kristen to drag her away. There were still about seven minutes before class, and the two girls found refuge in a grassy spot behind the library.

"Catie, you're coming unglued," Kristen scolded.

"I know! Ever since that chain letter, everything has fallen apart," Catie groaned.

"You think Triana sent you that chain letter?" Kristen asked.

"No. My sister sent it as a gag," Catie admitted. "But I told everybody about it, and I think maybe Triana heard me talking. Maybe she thought she could make all the misfortunes come true and the chain letter would be blamed. And that way I'd be too freaked to audition for the musical. Then Triana would walk off with the lead . . ."

"Catie, you don't *know* that any of that is true," Kristen pointed out. "Yeah, somebody is messing with you and your family, but it's not fair to just haul off and blame Triana when you don't have any proof."

"But why would anybody else do it? I don't have any enemies. I've always gotten along great with everybody, Kris. Triana has a good reason to sabotage my audition," Catie said.

"You've been reading too many mystery novels where everybody has a clear motive for doing what they do," said Kristen. "In the real world, some people just do stuff for no special reason. Maybe some sick, bored kid heard you talking about the chain letter on the bus that day and figured it'd be fun to make the bad-luck thing come true. You might not even know this person."

"Yeah," Catie finally admitted. "You're right, Kristen. I was out of line to accuse Triana like that. I made a big fool of myself. I'll apologize to Triana in math class."

"You better," Kristen said. "Come on now or we'll be late for math."

"Yeah," Catie said. "Ms. Bricker already thinks I'm a smoker. I don't want to give her reason to hate me even more!"

Catie and Kristen ran through campus until they got to the building where their algebra class was held. They managed to slide into their seats just as the tardy bell rang. Ms. Bricker gave Catie a stern look and proceeded to take roll.

Throughout the lesson on matrices, Catie kept glancing at Triana. Her face was red. Catie could tell she was still upset.

After class, Catie grabbed Triana's arm as she was walking out of the classroom. "Hey, Triana," she said, "I want to apologize for how I acted this morning. I didn't have the right to accuse you."

"Yeah, well, it's okay, I guess," Triana said. "In the future, just get your facts straight before you go around pointing fingers."

"Yeah," Catie said as Triana walked off. Catie felt bad for getting Triana so upset. Still, Triana had the best reason for messing with her than anyone else she could think of . . .

* * *

At lunch that noon, Catie found herself alone. She couldn't sit with Todd because of the animosity between them now. And Kristen had a club meeting. So Catie glanced around, looking for a familiar face. When she saw Ruben walking with his tray, she called out to him, "Hey, Ruben!"

Ruben grinned and came over, sitting opposite Catie. She had never eaten with him before. She felt bad remembering how she had always stuck with her own little group and often didn't want to include anybody else. When you were comfortable with your circle of friends, it sometimes spoiled things to include other people. That's how Catie felt, anyway.

"How's everything, Catie?" Ruben asked.

"Not very good," said Catie. "I had a big fight with Triana. I accused her of being behind this stuff that's been happening, and now I feel so stupid. I don't have any proof against her."

"Well, life gets rough sometimes," Ruben said. Most of the students at Marshall High knew that Ruben and his little brothers were in the middle of a bitter custody fight between their parents. Catie hadn't given it much thought when she first heard about it. She was too wrapped up in her own life. But now that she did think about it, she felt really sorry for Ruben. She thought how awful she felt that somebody on the outside was causing her trouble. She couldn't imagine how much worse she would feel if the trouble stemmed from a war between two people she loved, her parents.

"Did I tell you that somebody killed all my mom's roses, Ruben? Whoever it was came over at night and cut them down, then poured poison on the roots," Catie said.

"Sounds like somebody really hates you guys," Ruben said.

Catie was jarred by the word *hate*. It was scary. She preferred to think somebody with a twisted sense of humor was playing tricks on her. Or even that Triana was doing it to get the lead in the musical. But *hate*?

"Ruben, I've never done anything to make somebody hate me. How could that be?" she asked.

"I don't know, but I know hate when I see it," Ruben said. "My parents hate each other big-time. They've been doing really mean things to each other since the divorce. Like my dad really treasured his scrapbook with pictures of him and us kids from way back. His own childhood pictures were in there too, and his parents' pictures. Mom burned up the whole thing in the fireplace. Burned up all Dad's pictures. Dad felt so bad he cried like a little kid."

Catie was horrified. She tried to imagine how it would feel to lose all the photographs of happy family memories. "Can he replace any of the pictures?" she asked.

"No. Most of them were one of a kind," said Ruben. "Especially the ones of his family."

"Why does your mom hate your dad so much?" Catie asked.

"Because he doesn't love her anymore. He loves somebody else," Ruben said. "It's like he's throwing Mom away, see. He's taking their life together and bunching it up and throwing it away. And Mom feels betrayed and lost."

Catie was surprised that Ruben was revealing so much of his personal life. He'd never done that before. Catie thought he must feel really comfortable with her. She could understand that. She felt very much at ease with Ruben too.

"Mom says Dad has ruined her whole life," Ruben went on. "She said she'd be glad if she heard that he died."

"That must be terrible for you, Ruben," Catie said.

Ruben nodded. He looked steadily at Catie then. "I know hate when I see it or hear about it. Nobody would have pushed you in that closet and locked the door if they didn't hate you. Or maybe they hate your whole family. Maybe your mom or dad made some bad enemy. Anything is possible. You better be real careful, Catie."

Now Catie was really frightened. To think that there was somebody out there who hated her or her family, or both, was terrifying.

***

When the Rezo family sat down to dinner that night, Catie brought up the subject of all the misfortunes that had been happening. She recited them like a laundry list. She didn't mention that Leslie had written the chain letter though. She had promised she wouldn't, so she kept silent.

"Ruben thinks whoever is behind all this really hates me or hates our family," Catie said. "Do you guys have any enemies that you know of?" Catie looked at her parents.

Her mom set down her fork and looked totally bewildered. "Catie, I couldn't think of an enemy I have if someone paid me a million dollars. I've had small disagreements with people, but, my goodness, it all blew over, and now we're friends. I can't remember *ever* feeling any hatred," she said.

Catie's dad was equally confident that he didn't have any enemies. "We bid on different jobs, of course, and the guy who loses the bid probably isn't very happy. But hatred? No, I don't think so. It's preposterous," he said.

Suddenly a far-out thought occurred to Catie. "You know, Dad, I've got a friend at school whose parents are divorcing. There are really bitter feelings. You don't think that girl you divorced years ago is still feeling angry, do you?" she asked.

Her dad nearly spit out his iced tea. Laughing, he said, "Honey, it's been 17 years since I've even seen that girl. Alicia Monahan and I were stupid young kids who did a totally idiotic thing by running off and getting married. I'm sure she was as relieved as I was when the marriage was annulled."

Catie nodded. "Well, it was just a thought," she said. "I thought maybe she was pining away for you somewhere, all mad because she's old and bitter now and lost her first love."

"*Old* and bitter?" her dad pounced on the remark. "I will have you know, Catie, that Alicia and I are the same age, and that's not old. Your mother and I are just getting into the prime of life, dear daughter, so let's not have any more nonsense talk like that."

Catie's mom and dad both laughed. Her mom had called a gardener who was going to remove all the tainted soil in the rose garden, bring in fresh, healthy soil, and replant the garden with roses. She was willing to put the ugly incident behind her. Catie's dad was willing to forget about his slashed tires too. They were dismissing them as adolescent pranks. They didn't understand how it was for Catie at Marshall where ugly things kept happening.

***

When Catie arrived at school on Wednesday, Ruben was waiting for her near the entrance of the school. Catie smiled when she saw him.

"Hi, Catie. You busy on Saturday?" he asked.

"No, I don't think so," she said.

"Maybe you and I could go down to Ash River," he said. "It's about five miles from here. My family and I used to go there all the time and fish or just rent a rowboat and follow the river through the woods. There's a little restaurant at the bend in the river, and it's run by a Filipino family. They serve these really good egg rolls. We could make a nice day of it. We used to have a real good time there, before, you know, everything fell apart," Ruben explained. Catie knew that he was trying to make the place sound as inviting as possible so she would agree to go out with him. He didn't seem able to imagine that she might want to go because she enjoyed being with him.

"That sounds nice, Ruben," Catie said. She was desperate for something to divert her mind from what was happening.

Besides, she really was getting to like the guy she had ignored for so long. "I'd like to go."

Ruben brightened. "Okay! Then maybe I'll come to your house around 10:00 Saturday morning?" he asked.

"Yeah, sounds good," Catie said. Then she went on to class.

Catie knew she should not have agreed to go out with Ruben before she asked her parents. Since she was 16, it was okay with her parents if she went out on dates, but they wanted to know the boy first. Ruben was a stranger to them. He had never been to the house like Todd had. Catie had known Todd since they were both in middle school, and he was part of the group Catie usually hung out with. Catie had seen Ruben since middle school, but as an outsider.

***

When Catie got home from school, she told her mother about Ruben. "He's such a nice guy, Mom, and I've seen him around for a long time. He's the guy who drove me home the other day when I got pushed into the closet. He really came to my rescue. He asked me if I'd go down to Ash River on Saturday and just spend a few hours. I'd really like to go."

"I suppose it will be all right," her mom said. "But maybe he could come in and say hello before you go."

"Sure, Mom," Catie said.

Her mom was pretty agreeable about most things. And Catie knew she trusted Catie's judgment most of the time.

Catie studied history until about 10:00 that night, and then she went to bed. She was deep in sleep around midnight when she heard a terrible crash. The whole house seemed to shake. Catie leaped out of bed and ran to the front of the house. Her mom and dad were already there.

"Somebody threw a brick through the picture window, Catie," her dad said in a stunned voice.

Catie stared at the shattered front window, at the glass all over the pale green carpet.

"Oh, Catie . . ." her mom cried, "what's happening?"

8 After the police came and took a report, the Rezo family sat in the den. No one could go back to sleep right away, so they drank hot chocolate and talked.

"Catie, this is getting serious," her dad said. "There has to be some kid at Marshall who's doing this. Some boy with a crush on you. This has gone beyond weird pranks. Honey, a tarantula in your handbag is one thing, but slashed tires, your mother's destroyed garden, and now this. There has to be some punk down there at school who's acting out his frustration."

"I don't know who it would be, Dad," Catie said. "I know that Triana and I both want the lead in the school musical, but Triana surely wouldn't throw a brick through the window and maybe risk killing somebody!"

"What about Todd?" her dad asked pointedly. "You're not seeing him anymore, right? Could he be getting back at you?"

"All this trouble started long before Todd and I broke up, Dad," Catie said.

"*Think*, Catie," her dad said. "There's probably some boy at Marshall, some weird, little loner type who's been looking at you hopefully. You've probably ignored him, and now he's probably striking back . . ."

"Dad, honest, I can't think of anybody like that," Catie said. Of course maybe Ruben fit that category, but she and Ruben were going out on Saturday. Why would he heave a brick through the front window of her house now?

Leslie had been sitting quietly at the table sipping hot chocolate, but now she glanced up, a miserable look on her face. She turned and faced the window with cardboard taped over it. "It's all my fault," she said.

Their mom turned to Leslie. "What are you talking about, honey?" she asked. "How could this be your fault?"

"I sent Catie the chain letter. Paula and I dreamed it up. We had fun with a chain letter last year, and I thought this would be fun too. But it's not fun. It's horrible, and I'm so sorry." Tears started to roll down Leslie's cheeks. "I never knew such awful things could *really* happen if you didn't follow the instructions on a chain letter."

"Leslie, I'm terribly disappointed that you'd do something so stupid," her dad said in a harsh voice.

Leslie looked devastated. Catie knew that she loved their father so much. To be so harshly spoken to must be agony for her, Catie thought.

Leslie sobbed brokenly. Catie felt so sorry for her that she went over and tried to hug her. But her dad said sharply, "Leave her alone, Catie. Leslie, go to your room now. Think about what you have done. You obviously have too much time on your hands. Tomorrow we'll see if you're playing too many stupid computer games. You just might find yourself without a computer for the rest of the school year."

Leslie ran from the den and raced up the stairs to her room, crying all the way.

"It was just a silly prank, Martin," Catie's mom said. "The poor thing is really feeling bad. She thinks all these unfortunate incidents are her fault, and she needs to know the bad things have nothing to do with her chain letter." She stood and headed up the stairs after Leslie.

"You're too easy on her, Ellie," Catie's dad grumbled. "Much too easy."

"Dad, Leslie didn't mean to hurt anybody," Catie said.

Catie's dad shot her a hard look. "Catie, you're one of those mushy people like your mother. I've been worried about how many violent computer games your sister has been playing for a long time. Monsters with swords leaping at one another, blood and gore. Well, it's coming to an end now. No more games for that young lady."

Her dad had been more upset in the past couple weeks than Catie could ever remember him being. The harassment against the family was getting to him.

She couldn't blame her dad, though. It was getting to her too. But she decided not to mention to her father that she was going out with Ruben on Saturday. He didn't need anything else to worry about.

***

In history class on Friday, there was a discussion on the lack of trust so many people have in their government.

"My dad is always talking about those black helicopters," one boy said. "He thinks the government is watching us all the time."

Marty Jordan had been gone from school for several days. Now that she was back, Catie noticed that she seemed very glum. "I don't think there's any justice in this country," she said. "People who do really bad things get off real easy, and the little guy does a small crime, and they throw the book at him."

Catie was worried that maybe the theft case against Marty's mother had gone badly. So she caught up with Marty after class. She had been so kind in helping Catie that now Catie wanted to be there for her. "Marty, is everything okay at your house?" she asked.

Marty turned, a strange look on her face. She wasn't hysterical in the least, but she looked shocked. "My mother was arrested. They believed the old woman who said her jewelry had been taken. She's rich, you know."

"Oh, Marty, I'm so sorry," Catie said. "Are you . . . uh . . . with somebody else? I mean, are you okay?"

"The landlord evicted us then. Said he couldn't house any convicts. But I'm over 18. I have a little van, and that's where I'm staying now," Marty said.

In a burst of generosity, Catie said, "Marty, we have a spare guest room at our house. You're welcome to stay with us till everything is sorted out. I know Mom and Dad wouldn't mind."

Marty looked at Catie for a long moment. Then she said, "Are you sure?"

"Yeah," Catie said. "I'll call Mom right away and tell her. You can come home from school with me today."

Catie went to a pay phone and called her mom at the college. Catie explained all the problems Marty had been having and how she needed a place to stay for a while.

"Sure, Catie," her mom said. "Bring her home. Any of your friends are welcome in our house."

Catie ran back to Marty. "Mom said it's cool, Marty. We can go over and get your stuff."

"I'll drive over to your house around 5:00," Marty said. "That'll give me the chance to pack some stuff."

"Okay. See you then," Catie said.

***

Late that afternoon, just after 5:00, a beat-up, old van pulled in the driveway. Marty got out with a suitcase. "These are really nice houses in Juniper Hills," Marty said, staring down the street.

"Yeah. I was really excited when we moved in. Our old house was nice too, but this one is much better," Catie said.

"Your father must make really good money," Marty said.

"He does okay," Catie said. "We're not rich or anything, but Dad has a lot of business."

Marty was silent as she followed Catie up the walk. Her eyes were wide with admiration for the lovely house set behind pretty landscaping. Catie figured this house was far different from where Marty had lived.

Catie introduced Marty to her mother. Her mom was gracious as usual. "Nice to meet you, Marty. Catie is always bringing nice school friends home. Remember, sweetheart, when Kristen stayed with us for a month while her folks went to Europe?"

"Yeah," Catie said.

Catie led Marty up the stairs to the guest bedroom.

"Wow," Marty said, sizing up the room. "This is awesome. I've never had a room this nice before."

Catie felt really sorry for Marty. From what she had said, she lived a very difficult life. She said she lived in cars sometimes, drifting from place to place. And, worst of all, Marty never knew her dad. Catie couldn't imagine how hard that was. Even though Catie's dad could be stern sometimes, he was very important to her, and she loved him.

Marty sat down on the edge of the big bed and stared up at the rose-colored ceiling fan. "Imagine, if I had a different family, then I'd live in a place like this all the time," she said in a faraway voice. "It's all about where you're born and who you're born to, right? I mean, that's what your life is . . ."

"But that isn't how your life always has to be," Catie pointed out. "You can get an education, find a good job, and have a nice life for yourself."

Marty didn't comment on what Catie had said. She just kept looking around the room in wonder. "Sometimes I'd cut pictures of pretty houses out of magazines and put them in a scrapbook. I'd show the pictures to Mom and ask her if real people lived in those houses. But she'd always say no, that they were just pictures and they didn't mean anything. Mom told me just a tiny group of rich people lived in really nice houses," Marty said.

"This is just an ordinary house," Catie said. "It's not a palace or anything. A lot of people live in houses like this."

***

The next day Catie was worried about leaving Marty to go have lunch with Ruben, but Marty said she was fine. Catie's mom had promised to give Marty a piano lesson, and then they were going to make whatever Marty wanted for lunch. Catie's mom seemed really eager to make Marty feel at home, and Catie was grateful for that.

Catie's dad had said he would help get Marty settled too. Catie had caught Marty staring at her dad a few times the previous evening. Sometimes Catie wished she had a normal dad. It was kind of embarrassing to have a dad who was so handsome.

Right on time, Ruben pulled into the driveway. He came into the house and was very affable to Catie's parents. Catie was impressed. She thought he was unusually polite for a teenage guy. He even talked to her dad about his favorite sport— basketball. For a shy guy, Ruben did really well, Catie thought.

As Catie and Ruben drove toward Ash River, Catie told him about having Marty over for a few days. "She's all alone now," Catie said. "I thought she needed a friend until her mother gets this straightened out."

Ruben shook his head. "I think Marty's

mom is going to get hard time. My cousin does landscaping for the lady she stole from, and it looks like she did take a lot of good stuff," he said.

"Oh, wow, poor Marty," Catie said.

"Yeah. Those cleaning ladies don't make much money, so you can see why she was tempted to steal stuff," Ruben said. "It wasn't right, but you can see how it happens."

"That's so sad," Catie said.

"It's nice you took her in, though," added Ruben.

When they got to the river, Ruben rented a little rowboat. "Most people like motorboats, but I prefer to row. It makes you feel part of the river when you just go silently with the current," he said.

They both climbed into the boat. Ruben then rowed into the middle of the river where the boat caught the current.

"I've been wanting to take you out since I was 14," Ruben said, his dark, engaging eyes staring into Catie's. "I liked you so much. Remember when I asked you to the freshman dance?"

Catie smiled and nodded. "I remember."

The boat moved slowly with the current. "And then last year I asked you to a movie, and you said no again," Ruben remembered. "You said you were hanging out with Todd. But I didn't give up. I'm a pretty stubborn guy. I thought if I kept at it, eventually you'd go out with me." A smile turned Ruben's lips. "My grandma says good luck can be bad luck, and bad luck can be good luck. So all the bad luck you've been having . . . it was good luck for me. If you'd never been locked in that closet and scared so badly, I couldn't have offered you a ride home. Then we wouldn't be together now. So the bad luck was sorta good luck . . ."

Catie felt funny. Ruben was staring at her with his dark blue-black eyes, a triumphant smile on his lips. Catie remembered what her dad had said about some loner perhaps harassing her just to get her attention.

Could Ruben have been behind the troubling incidents? Was that his way of throwing her into his arms?

And now Catie was in a rowboat in the middle of a river with him . . .

9 Catie firmly pushed the suspicion from her mind. She looked at the cute, nice guy sitting across from her. Ruben could never have done those hurtful things to her, she thought. It just wasn't possible.

Along the brushy riverbanks, blue herons flew from the tree branches. Owls rested, waiting for darkness.

"It's beautiful here," Catie said.

"Yeah, I always liked it here," Ruben said. "It's hard to believe the desert's not far from here. That's why Mom always liked to come, to get away from the dryness." He changed the subject then. "When is the audition for the school musical?"

"In a week. I talked to Mr. Baron, and he told me it'd be a week from Wednesday," Catie said.

"You've got a really nice voice. I bet you win," Ruben said. "You blew me away in the sophomore talent show."

"That's sweet of you to say, Ruben," Catie said. "I've grown up loving music. Mom and Dad took me to my first opera when I was like five or six. I just loved it. The elaborate costumes, the lights, the excitement. It was just so bright and thrilling, almost like a circus."

They rowed to the shoreline at lunchtime and ordered egg rolls at the little restaurant. Catie loved the food. In fact, she thought the whole afternoon was wonderful.

Catie realized that she enjoyed being with Ruben much more than she had ever enjoyed being with Todd. He was down-to-earth and easy to be with. Todd was always talking about himself or what interested him. When Catie was with Todd, they always talked about his successes, football, his ideas about everything. He was the star of every conversation. But when Catie and Ruben talked, they kicked topics back and forth.

When Ruben took Catie home that day, Catie said, "I really enjoyed today. I didn't think I'd have so much fun."

"Yeah, me too," Ruben said with a warm smile.

Then he grabbed her hand and pulled her toward him. Catie closed her eyes as his warm lips pressed against hers. Then she climbed out of the pickup and ran inside, her heart pounding.

When Catie went inside, she was a little nervous about what mood Marty would be in. Maybe she had felt abandoned by Catie. Maybe she had had problems with Catie's mom or dad.

"Hi. I'm home," Catie called out.

But nobody answered. Catie threw down her purse by the front door and looked around. Then, suddenly, Marty appeared in the doorway between the living room and the den. "Your parents went out. They'll be back in a couple hours," she said.

Catie was surprised that her mom and dad would just leave a houseguest all by herself. It wasn't like them. "Oh? Where's Leslie?" Catie asked.

"Oh, she went with them. I promised to hold down the fort. Did you and Ruben have a nice time?" Marty asked.

"Yeah, we did. He's really cool," Catie said, sitting down on the sofa. "Did Mom give you a piano lesson?"

"Uh huh," Marty said. "But I didn't like it. I don't think I'd ever be good at music. You gotta get started when you're young, like a little kid."

Catie felt uneasy. There was something wrong with Marty. She wouldn't sit down. She fidgeted and darted around the room nervously. She'd sit for a moment on the arm of a chair, then rest on the corner of a table for a second. "You okay, Marty?" Catie asked quizzically.

"Sure," Marty said. "As okay as I'll ever be," she laughed.

"Your mom . . . are you allowed to see her—" Catie began.

"She's not really my mom," Marty said. "She's my foster mom. Her last name's *Jordan*. I was just using it."

"Oh," Catie said, surprised. "Where's your real mom?"

Marty played with a string she had in her hand. She was silent for a few minutes, then she said. "Oh, she's dead. She died three weeks ago."

"Oh, Marty! How awful," Catie cried. Marty had appeared at Marshall High just two weeks ago. It must have been just after her mother's death. "You must be hurting so much . . . your mom . . ."

Marty was surprisingly unemotional. She shrugged and said, "She was in a hospice. We knew she was gonna die. I've been living with my foster mom for three years. My mom, my real mom, she was really pretty, but she had such a bad life. It was all downhill. Sometimes we went down slow, and sometimes real fast, but it was always downhill. She never got over my father. Some people can have a whole string of boyfriends, but they never get over one. They're like stuck in love or something. That was Mom. She drank and did drugs to forget. That's what killed her in the end . . ."

"That's so sad," Catie said.

Marty glanced around the room. "She never in her whole life lived in a house like this. She never had good stuff. Our furniture was all junk from thrift shops. Like she got this cheapie cabinet to put her collectibles in, but they weren't good things. They were from the dollar store. She'd get some piece of trash and bring it home and put it in the cabinet, like it was something, but it was nothing." Marty crossed the room to a beautiful ceramic sculpture. "Like, look at this piece here. I bet it was really expensive."

"Well, yeah," Catie said.

Marty reached out and took the piece in her hands. She turned it around for different views. Then she said, "I told your parents when they were outside in the garden that your grandmother had called to come visit her because she was sick. I heard them talking about a grandmother in Briartown, so I thought they'd believe me. That's where they are . . . I really didn't get a call. It was a lie," Marty said. She laughed again.

Catie turned numb. Something was wrong. Something was terribly wrong. "Marty, what's going on? Why did you tell my parents that?"

Marty smiled again. She held the sculpture high over her head and cast it violently into the stone fireplace. The sculpture smashed into a hundred shards.

"Marty!" Catie cried in horror. "That was Dad's anniversary gift to my mom!" she cried.

"My mom never got an anniversary gift," Marty answered shrilly. "Not even a stinking box of cheap chocolates, okay? Is that fair? What's the big deal about *your* mother? My mother was just as good as your mother. My mother was pretty and sweet too. She held me in her arms and sang lullabies to me, even when we lived like dirt. Why didn't she get a nice house to live in and a nice husband to love her?" Marty was gasping with angry emotion now. "And who do you think you are? Why didn't I get a father to *love me*?"

Catie was shocked and frightened. She was trying to decide how dangerous Marty was and if she should try to make a run for it. Then the phone rang.

Marty snatched up the large dagger-like letter opener from the coffee table and cried in a threatening voice, "Don't tell anybody what's going on here. *I'm warning you!*"

10

"Hey, Catie, it's Ruben," said the voice on the other end of the line. "Want to go down to the El Dorado tomorrow and listen to some friends and me play some classic rock?"

"I can't talk now. I'm busy," Catie said in a strained voice. Marty was glaring at her.

"Are you okay, Catie?" Ruben asked. Catie couldn't tell if he could discern that anything was wrong from the tone of her voice or not. She hoped so . . .

"No," Catie said. "Good-bye."

"Who was that?" Marty demanded when Catie hung up.

"A telemarketer," Catie lied.

"You know, I think I'll smash everything in this house, and then I'll set it on fire," Marty said.

"Marty, I know you're hurting, but you can't do stuff like that," Catie pleaded.

"Why not? I have just as much right to be here as you. It's not your house any more than it's my house, and I can do what I want," Marty said.

"Marty—" Catie groaned.

"I did it all, you know. I wanted to do something to you and your family to make it even somehow, because it isn't fair. Why should you have this happy, secure family, and all I have is a dead mother? I overheard your friends talking about the stupid chain letter, and I thought, 'That's great. They'll blame it all on that. I can make war on the Rezo family, and they'll blame the chain letter.' So I put my tarantula in your purse and sicced my dog on you. I pushed you in the closet and told the teachers lies about you." Marty began to laugh in a manic way. "I slashed the tires on your truck and killed your mother's pretty roses. I wanted to make your family as miserable as mine has always been . . ."

"Marty—why?" Catie gasped.

"Because he's my father too," Marty said.

Catie felt as if she would faint. "What are you saying?" she asked.

"Martin William Rezo is my father. My

mother told me his name before she died. She said I didn't have anybody now, so I should look him up," Marty said.

"Marty—that's impossible—there's a mistake," Catie cried. And then she stared more closely at Marty. Her eyes grew wide in horror. She could see her father's features in Marty. She had never noticed it before because she wasn't looking for it. "Marty—was Alicia Monahan your mother?" she whispered.

"Uh huh," Marty said. She stared at a crystal vase. Her voice was hard and cold. "When my father told my mother he thought the marriage was a mistake, she went along with it. She was a wimp. But she never got over him. She never told him he had a daughter. 'I don't want to mess up his life,' she had said. But, oh, now it's vengeance time!"

Suddenly there was a knock on the door. Marty stared at the door, wide-eyed. "Go away!" she cried.

But the front door wasn't locked, so Ruben stepped in. He looked from Catie to Marty, and then he stared at the smashed sculpture in the fireplace.

"Catie's father is my father too," Marty said, a faraway look in her eyes. "But he never fathered me. He never knew Mom and me when we lived like dogs and ate out of trash bins. He never saw Mom fall into her drunken stupor, and he never comforted me when I dragged her home. I never knew until three weeks ago who my father was. But now I know. And now Martin William Rezo's pretty family is going to pay!" She grabbed for a crystal vase to pitch it into the fireplace too, but Ruben reached her in one long stride and grabbed her.

"Marty, I hear where you're coming from," he said. "I know what it's like when your home is no good, and everybody is fighting and screaming, and you're not safe . . ."

Marty fought and escaped Ruben's grasp. She made a quick dash to the other side of the room. Grabbing a table lamp, she threw it onto the hardwood floor, shattering it.

Catie shook. She knew the sculpture and the lamp could be replaced. But she was worried about when Marty was going to start turning her anger on her or Ruben.

"You don't know!" Marty screamed at Ruben. "Nobody knows!"

Catie slowly walked backward, away from Marty, while Ruben slowly inched his way toward her. Catie could see that his eyes were fixed on Marty. But they weren't angry eyes or scared eyes. They were compassionate. Catie could tell that he really wanted to help the hurting girl.

Ruben continued speaking in a soothing voice. "My mom says she wishes my dad were dead," he told Marty. "I know what it's like to feel like your heart is being ripped out."

Marty's shoulders were relaxing a bit as Ruben spoke. Catie sensed that her anger was abating. "Listen, Marty," he continued, "you're hurting. But what good does it do to hurt others? It won't make you feel better. My mom's trying to feel better by hurting my dad, but she's just hurting herself more. She's becoming dead inside herself. Come on, Marty, let us help you. It's okay to feel angry. It's okay to feel sad. You just have to trust us that we want to help."

Finally Marty's rage turned to sobs. Her grip on the letter opener loosened, and it dropped to the floor. Catie noticed that it took a little chunk out of one of the cherry-wood boards.

"Listen," Ruben continued, now only a foot or so from her, "we're young, Marty. We can do better than the place we came from. We can build a good life where it's warm and safe for *our* kids. You'll meet a guy, and it'll be good for you. Just because our parents failed us, that's no reason we can't have a good future. We're young. We can do it. We have another chance for a warm, safe place to live . . ."

Marty crumbled then, and Ruben grabbed her before she collapsed on the hard floor. He held her as she cried tears that had been pent up for 19 years. He looked over and winked at Catie then. His wink told her to be cool, to let him take Marty somewhere to cry it all out. *It will be all right now*, Ruben's warm, dark eyes promised. He gently guided Marty upstairs where she could lie down.

Catie cleaned up the broken statue and lamp. Then she sat down and waited for her parents to come home. She ached with sorrow at the life her dad's first love had lived. But her dad did not know. He had gone off to the army, and he never knew because Alicia never told him.

She was upset with Marty for causing all the problems in her life, but she knew her own short-lived stress was nothing compared to the stress Marty had felt her entire life.

Marty's past was a tragedy, but Marty's future could be changed. Soft, warm tears ran down Catie's face. Marty needed help, and Catie knew her family would do what they could for Marty. Her dad would try to make it up to the daughter he never knew. Catie knew he would. And she would try to be a sister to Marty, if Marty ever let her. Perhaps one day they might even be close.

Catie remembered the adage Ruben had shared with her on the boat. Now it rang truer than ever. And it gave her a glimmer of hope and a fresh perspective on the ordeal she had just been through.

Bad luck could sometimes turn into good luck.